Donkey in Distress

Peter Clover

ILLUSTRATED BY

Carolyn Dinan

OXFORD
UNIVERSITY PRESS

OXFORD
UNIVERSITY PRESS

Great Clarendon Street, Oxford OX2 6DP

Oxford University Press is a department of the University of Oxford.
It furthers the University's objective of excellence in research, scholarship,
and education by publishing worldwide in

Oxford New York

Auckland Bangkok Buenos Aires Cape Town
Chennai Dar es Salaam Delhi Hong Kong Istanbul Karachi
Kolkata Kuala Lumpur Madrid Melbourne Mexico City Mumbai
Nairobi São Paulo Shanghai Singapore Taipei Tokyo Toronto

with an associated company in Berlin

Oxford is a registered trade mark of Oxford University Press
in the UK and in certain other countries

British Library Cataloguing in Publication Data available

ISBN 0-19-275260-X

1 3 5 7 9 10 8 6 4 2

Designed and Typeset by Mike Brain Graphic Design Limited, Oxford

Printed in Great Britain by Cox & Wyman Ltd, Reading, Berkshire

Whistlewind Farm is a fictional donkey sanctuary and the practises described, although authentic,
are not based on those used by any real donkey sanctuary.

To the real Jenny Lester,
Peter, Daisy and Poppy

All the books in this series have been read and approved
by the Folly's Farm Sanctuary for Donkeys.

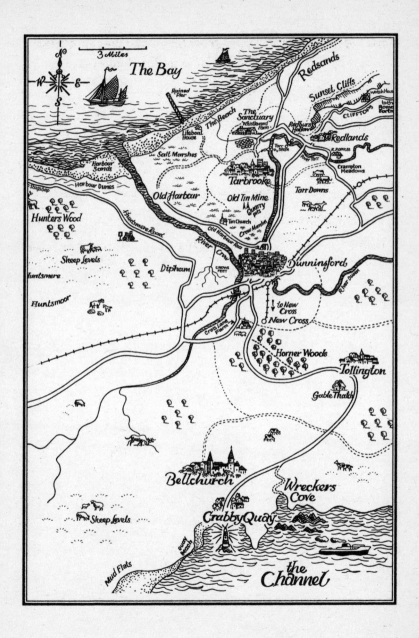

It was half-term, and Danni was helping out at her parents' donkey sanctuary.

'Any news?' she asked.

Kristie raised her eyebrows, then shook her head. Kristie Blythe was seventeen and, like Danni, she was bonkers about donkeys.

Kristie worked with Danni's parents, Jenny and Peter Lester, at The Sanctuary in Tarbrooke — a donkey retreat, devoted to providing loving care to rescued and unwanted donkeys.

Kristie ran a hand through her long, curly mane of fiery, copper hair and led Houdini back in from the grazing paddock.

'Jenny said they'd telephone as soon as they got there,' she added.

Suddenly, Houdini went on strike. He dug in his hooves and refused to move any further.

Danni laughed. 'He wants to stay in there with the others.'

'I know he does,' agreed Kristie. 'But he's being very naughty. Clever-clogs has discovered

1

a loose fence post and you know what he's like. He won't leave it alone until he's worried it right out of the ground. So *he's* coming out, instead.'

'But that's what Houdini does best,' grinned Danni. 'He escapes.'

'Well, not today he doesn't,' countered Kristie. 'At least, not while I've been left in charge! He can sulk in the welcome pen and wait for Jenny and Peter to come back with the new resident.'

The Lester's liked to call their donkeys residents. It somehow made them seem more permanent. Like part of a real family.

Kristie pulled gently on Houdini's head

collar, but the stubborn donkey was an old hand at this. He wasn't going anywhere.

'Hee yaawwwww!!' he protested noisily.

'You're definitely going to need these,' said Danni. She peeled open a tube of peppermints and waved them in front of Houdini's nose. The donkey's hairy nostrils twitched and his long furry ears waggled like a giant rabbit's.

'Attaboy,' coaxed Kristie as Houdini shuffled forward, feigning defeat. 'Go and get your bribe. That's it. Nice and slowly. Easy does it. Don't rush yourself!'

Houdini was no fool. He knew the mints would come out eventually. The glint in his eyes told Danni that!

Just then, Kristie's mobile rang. It was Jenny Lester, Danni's mum.

Huntsmere Downs — Dipham

'We're here,' said Jenny. 'But it looks a bit trickier than we thought. I'll ring again later

3

when we've got more news.' Then she hung up the phone.

Peter Lester had backed up the truck as close to the ditch as possible, and kicked two big rocks behind the rear tyres. They were in the rescue pick-up. The big truck with the winch on the back.

Jenny crouched low at the top of the ditch and reached out to the trapped donkey.

'Oh, you poor thing!' Her voice was soft and soothing. 'We'll soon have you out of there!'

The donkey raised its shaggy head above the muddy water-line and let out a pathetic bray. Its nostrils were clogged with mud. Its breathing was shallow and laboured.

The donkey was stuck up to its shoulders in thick, muddy, ditch-water. No matter how frantically it struggled, it couldn't climb out.

'Poor thing could have been here for days,' said Peter. 'It's a good job those hikers came by and called us at The Sanctuary.'

'There, there,' said Jenny calmly. Her hand softly brushed the donkey's cheek and offered comfort. She stroked the matted neck and slipped into the mucky water beside the petrified animal. Her feet sank into the squelchy, slimy mud. And the cold water rose up to her armpits.

The poor donkey made no attempt to struggle or move away. It was frozen with fear. Jenny carefully felt all over the donkey's body. She ran her hands across its back, loins, and flanks. Then she reached beneath the muddy water and felt its belly.

'What's wrong?' asked Peter urgently. He could tell from Jenny's face that something wasn't quite right.

'She's extremely weak,' replied Jenny. 'Like we thought . . . she must have been here for several days.' There was a long pause. 'She's also in foal. And I think it's due, really soon.'

The Sanctuary — Whistlewind Farm

Tim Bentley came pedalling up the gravel drive at 100 mph. Shingle exploded from his tyres in all directions as he seared a lightning path to The Sanctuary.

'Are they here yet?' he yelled, spinning his wheels and skidding to a halt in the main yard.

Shadow, Danni's black racing donkey, threw up his head in greeting. 'Hee yawwww!!!' he bellowed. Shadow had a voice like a foghorn and liked to use it as often as possible.

Danni had put Shadow in with Houdini to keep him company. But Houdini was still sulking. He was still thinking about his nice wobbly post, and totally ignoring the little black dynamo.

'Hi, Shad,' chirped Tim. 'Where is everyone?'

'We're here,' echoed a chorus of two voices as Danni and Kristie ambled out of the isolation barn with armfuls of straw. They were preparing the barn for the new arrival.

'Apparently, it's a bit trickier than they first thought,' began Danni. 'We don't know exactly what's happening yet, but if Mum says it's tricky, then it must be bad!'

'But if anyone can rescue a donkey,' enthused Kristie, 'Jenny can. I'm sure everything's fine and they'll phone again, soon.'

'I'll give you a hand,' said Tim. But first, he leant over the five-bar gate, scratched Shadow's furry ears, and rubbed the grateful donkey under his whiskery chin, just on the spot where he loved it best. 'What's up with Houdini?'

'Sulking,' grinned Danni. 'He's masterminded a new escape route, and Kristie's nipped his plan in the bud. Wobbly post syndrome! Ever heard of it?'

Tim laughed. But Houdini didn't think it was very funny. As if he had understood every word, the naughty donkey picked up an empty feed bucket with his teeth and tossed it over the fence.

The tin pail landed with a clatter at their feet.

'Oh, by the way,' laughed Danni, 'that's his new trick. Bucket bombing!'

Huntsmere Downs — Dipham

'It looks like we've got two options,' said Peter. He wiped a smear of mud from his forehead and studied the problem. 'We can either lay planks in the ditch and try to ease her up a makeshift ramp. Or, use the sling and lift her clean out with the winch on the truck.'

'The donkey's condition makes either way dangerous,' worried Jenny. 'She's so weak. Getting her to struggle up a ramp will take a lot of effort. She's already exhausted!'

'Lifting her out might be the best solution,' said Peter. 'But her entire weight will be supported by the sling . . .'

'. . . and the sling goes right around, under her belly,' finished Jenny. 'She's heavy with the foal. I'm not sure!'

'Either way,' said Peter. 'She can't stay where she is. She'll surely die. We've got to do something. And we've got to do it now!'

'Then we'll risk lifting her out,' concluded Jenny. 'I honestly don't think she would make it

up a muddy ramp. One slip and she'd be finished.'

Peter agreed and slipped into the ditch alongside Jenny. The donkey turned her head and nosed his shirt. She seemed to know that they were trying to help. She made no sound as Peter slipped the canvas sling beneath her rounded belly. He tightened the straps across the donkey's rear and fastened the supporting bib across her chest.

'I'll try and adjust the harness to lift more

from the withers,' said Peter. Then he scrambled up the bank out of the ditch.

Moments later, the winch kicked into life and the sling began to lift the little donkey to safety.

At first, she panicked slightly as the canvas tightened around her middle. But then she felt her feet pulling free from the sticky mud. And suddenly she was being lifted out of the murky ditch-water. She hung her head and brayed softly. There wasn't an ounce of fight left in her.

It took less than a minute to complete the rescue. Once on firm ground, Jenny and Peter got busy with towels and old blankets. They rubbed the little donkey all over, from head to hoof. Apart from her swollen belly, she was so thin and bony. The rubbing helped the donkey's blood to circulate and pump round her body. It made her feel much warmer.

They wrapped her in layers of thick, dry blankets, then gently encouraged her up the short ramp into the back of their little pony trailer.

10

'Let's go,' said Jenny. Like Peter, she was freezing and soaked through to the skin. But she didn't care. She climbed up into the truck and grabbed a towel. 'Nice and easy does it,' she smiled. 'Let's get this poor baby back to The Sanctuary as quickly and smoothly as possible.'

Tarr Downs — Tarbrooke

A horse and rider shot out of the copse like a bullet fired from a gun. The horse had bolted. Its ears lay flat against its head. Nostrils were flared. Its eyes were showing white and filled with fear. The horse ran full out at a mad gallop. It was obviously terrified and out of control.

The rider was also in a desperate panic. Hanging on for grim death, he was bouncing about all over the place. He yelled and screamed into the facing wind. He yanked on the leather reins. But the horse streaked on, terrified of the screeching pheasant in the trees,

11

which had spooked it in the first place. The horse was desperate to get away and free itself from the lumpy rider on its back.

Pounding hooves thundered across the hard ground. The rider raised his arm — not for the first time that day — and brought the riding crop slashing down, with a noisy crack, across the horse's rump. It was cruel and possibly the worst thing he could have done. The horse was already half out of its mind with fear. It had nowhere to run but forwards. And now, all it could do was go faster, as the vicious crop struck again and again.

The hedgerow loomed quickly. One minute there was a clear run ahead. Then an enormous leap as the horse took the rider up and over the hedge. The next obstacle was a wooden fence. The fence marked the boundary of The Sanctuary at Whistlewind Farm.

This time the rider almost left the saddle as the horse took the jump. He slipped to the right but managed, somehow, to hold on to a fistful of wild mane. The rider's misplaced weight made

the horse falter and clip the top bar of the fence
as it sailed over. The wooden rail splintered
across the horse's front legs as it landed in the
grassy paddock.

There were eight donkeys in that paddock.
Eight donkeys which scattered to the far
corners of their grazing field as the horse and
rider came charging through.

The donkeys watched in horror as the horse
stormed past. Moments later they brayed in
alarm as the horse missed its footing at the next
jump and crashed into the heavy fencing. Its
forelegs crumpled beneath it. Its nose hit the

concrete slabs of the yard. And the poor horse somersaulted right over. The rider had been thrown to one side and was already getting to his feet. The horse was up, too. But it wasn't moving. It stood quite still, trembling with fear.

The Sanctuary — Whistlewind Farm

Danni Lester, Tim, and Kristie watched with their mouths hanging open. None of them could believe their eyes. One minute they were calmly preparing the isolation barn for a new arrival, and the next thing, they were gawping in horror at a rider on a runaway horse as it crashed through The Sanctuary fence.

The eight donkeys in the grazing paddock were braying at the top of their lungs. They trembled in a huddled corner, too afraid to move. Other donkeys in the adjacent field came rushing over to see what all the fuss was about. Donkeys in stables poked their heads over the half-doors and joined in the noisy chorus.

14

In the middle of all this confusion stood the terrified horse. It held one injured foreleg in the air, gently pawing it back and forth. Its chest and shins were ripped and bleeding. The poor animal was shaking like a leaf. White foam dribbled from its mouth and hung in long strings. The horse was absolutely panic stricken and frozen with fright.

Luckily, the rider wasn't injured. Only his pride seemed to be hurt. Within seconds of brushing down his torn jacket he grabbed at the horse's dangling reins. His face was set, like a mask fixed with an angry sneer. His free hand still gripped the leather riding crop. He raised the whip in a nasty rage and began beating the injured horse.

Less than one minute had passed since the horse had crashed through the fencing. It was like a bad dream. It all seemed so unreal. Danni, Tim, and Kristie hadn't moved. Until now. Suddenly the spell was broken, as Danni found her voice.

'Stop that!' she screamed. 'Stop it!!' Then

she flew at the man. Tim and Kristie were with her immediately.

'Leave him alone!' Kristie grabbed the rider's arm. Tim snatched the crop and flung it away. The horse reared up in panic. The rider yanked at the reins, jerking the proud head down.

'Gerroff me!' he yelled angrily. 'Mind your own business and leave me alone.'

Kristie struggled with the rider. 'Just let the horse go,' she ordered. Tim charged in and pushed the man away. Danni quickly gathered the reins and managed to gain control of the animal. She led the horse away out of harm's reach. The first place she could think of to take him was the isolation barn. It was nice and quiet in there.

Danni led him inside while Kristie tried to reason with the irate rider.

'I'm going to have that stupid lump put down and sold for horse-meat,' he threatened at the top of his voice. 'It's useless. A broken bundle of nerves. Anyone can see that. Spooked by a stupid bird in the woods. He's finished. No good to anyone. I'm going to drag him off to the knacker's yard, right now!'

'Oh no you're not,' said Kristie. 'He's staying right here.'

'Over my dead body,' argued the man. 'I'm taking him. And I'm taking him right now!'

But before he had time to push Kristie aside, move a single muscle . . . or say another word, he was hit by a flying object. Houdini's tin pail clattered to the ground as the man sank to his knees. He had just been 'bucket bombed' by you-know-who.

'Hee Hawwwwwww!!!'

The Sanctuary — five minutes later

The vet was trying to stay calm as he bandaged Lance Parker's head. Lance Parker was Houdini's victim and owner of the injured

17

horse. He was furious. And he was threatening to sue Kristie and The Sanctuary for assault.

'You haven't heard the last of this,' he mumbled.

Luckily, Jenny had called the vet en route from Dipham, and asked him to come to The Sanctuary as soon as he could. She wanted the vet to be there when she arrived with the pregnant donkey. The vet had been in the area visiting a neighbouring farm and had arrived early. Which was lucky for Lance Parker.

The rider had calmed down a bit when he saw the vet. But he was still angry. Lance Parker was a bully by nature. Teenage girls, children, and nervous horses were easier to push around than a grown man. Lance Parker also had a thumping great headache. And a bump the size of a grapefruit.

'I think I'll just take a look at that horse while I'm waiting for Jenny,' suggested the vet.

'You leave him alone,' snapped Lance Parker. 'That horse is going for meat. I don't need any fancy vet's bills to pay on top. I want him destroyed. I'm going to pay you to put him down not examine him.'

His nasty words hung silently in the air like a poisoned balloon. Moments later, the Lesters' pick-up truck and trailer crunched up the gravel drive into The Sanctuary.

'What's going on?' asked Jenny. 'Where's Danni?' Her eyes met Lance Parker's. Jenny didn't like the look of him at all.

'And just who exactly are you?' he demanded in return.

Jenny's eyes flashed.

'Introductions later,' she replied flatly. 'I've something more important on my hands at the moment.' She shot a grateful glance at the vet. 'We've brought in a pregnant donkey about to give birth. Poor thing's exhausted and totally dehydrated. Is the barn ready, Kristie?'

Kristie quickly explained everything. Jenny liked Lance Parker even less after that.

'I'll check the donkey over in the trailer,' suggested the vet. 'It might be best in the long run if we don't move her.'

'And I'll look in on the horse,' offered Peter.

'Leave that horse alone,' hissed Lance Parker. 'I've already gone over that issue. He's my property and no one's to go anywhere near him.'

Jenny turned smartly on her heels. She squared up to Lancer Parker and met him face to face.

'This is Sanctuary property,' she said sternly. Her brows were knitted together. Jenny meant business. 'And we shall go anywhere we please. I also suggest that you leave immediately before I call the police to remove you.'

'I'm not going anywhere without my horse,' retaliated Lance Parker.

'The horse is staying here for the moment,' insisted Jenny. 'At least until the vet has examined him thoroughly.'

'You can't do that! I forbid it. I'll have you all arrested.'

'Arrested!' smiled Jenny. 'I don't think so. Cruelty to animals is a very serious offence around here. Rest assured, it will be you who is arrested. Make no mistake about that! Besides,' she added. 'You said that you wanted him to be destroyed and sold as horse meat. We'll keep the horse and pay you the going rate.'

Lance Parker suddenly fell silent.

'How do I get to Crampton Meadows from here?' he demanded.

'I'll run you into Tarbrook,' said Jenny. 'You can get a taxi from there.'

The isolation barn

Danni stood and watched as Peter examined the horse. She had already taken a good look herself, and treated the cuts and gashes with an old-fashioned, country remedy . . . cobwebs. In an emergency, fresh cobwebs laid across a wound stops the bleeding. And it had worked a treat.

Danni held the horse's head while Peter looked at its injured leg. Sweat was running

down its arched neck. It was obvious that the
horse was in a great deal of pain. His foreleg
was already swelling up like a balloon.

'I think he may have pulled a tendon,' said
Peter. 'I don't think it's broken.'

Danni stayed with the horse while her dad
went to fetch the vet. She promised the horse

that he would soon feel better. But the horse was in too much distress to listen. The skin on his poor leg was stretched so taught, it looked ready to burst.

'That man is horrible,' said Danni, when Peter came back with the vet. 'He wants to have this beautiful animal destroyed. We won't let him, will we, Dad?'

Peter smiled. 'Not if your mother has anything to do with it!'

Inside the pony trailer

'How is she?' asked Peter.

'She's in the very first stages of labour,' replied the vet. 'So it shouldn't be long.' But the vet looked worried. 'It doesn't look good, I'm afraid. It's going to be a breech birth.'

'Oh, no,' gasped Danni. 'The poor thing. She must have been through so much already.'

'What's a breech birth?' whispered Tim. He was stroking the donkey's head and giving it some TLC [Tender Loving Care]. The donkey responded by lipping at his hand.

'A breech birth means that the foal is going to come out backwards,' explained Danni.

'This poor donkey's foal is completely twisted the wrong way round,' said the vet.

Tim gave Danni a worried glance. 'I've never seen anything being born before,' he said. 'Apart from on TV.'

Danni nudged him in the ribs. It was hard to imagine that a new life was about to appear and take its place in the world. Tim prayed that everything would be all right.

'Is it OK if we stay?' asked Danni.

'As long as you keep quiet,' smiled the vet. 'And keep out of the way.'

Danni and Tim hugged each other and settled down in a corner of the trailer. The pregnant donkey lay down on the soft bedding of straw.

'Now then, my girl,' smiled the vet. He laid a gentle hand on the donkey's stomach. 'Let's see if we can do this together.'

Somehow, the vet had to try and turn the foal around into the correct position. He explained everything to Kristie as he worked. Danni and Tim tried to picture in their heads what he was doing.

The donkey half lifted her head and gave a huge sigh. She was sweating a lot and Kristie was bathing her face and neck with a damp rag.

'Hang in there, my beauty,' whispered Kristie. 'It will soon be over.'

The vet was trying his best to correct the breech, but it wasn't working. Minutes dragged past and there was still no progress. Jenny had once told Danni that unlike human babies, foals are usually born very quickly. It was only because of the breech birth that it was taking this long.

'It's no good,' exclaimed the vet, finally. He looked up at Kristie. 'I hate to say this, but I think we're going to lose the foal.'

A huge wave of hopelessness swept through the trailer. Danni gripped Tim's hand. 'Please, please, don't let it die,' she whispered to herself.

Outside in the yard, a small group of donkeys had gathered around the trailer. Queenie, Ethel, Poppy, Daisy, Dixie, Rosie, and Jude — all female donkeys — huddled together and worried in low tones. They seemed to know that something was wrong and set up a low, wheezing bray. It sounded like soft bleating. A warm, comforting sound which hummed inside the trailer.

The pregnant donkey raised her head. Her ears twitched as she listened to the braying. She tried to respond. But it was tough. Her cry came out as a tired 'Yawwww!' Yet knowing that the other donkeys were outside seemed to give her strength.

The vet went back to work. Everyone else waited. Danni and Tim held their breath as the minutes ticked by. Then suddenly, huge grins spread across their faces. Danni's eyes grew to the size of saucers. It was so beautiful. It was the foal. And it was being born.

'She's done it,' whispered Tim. 'She's done it.'

The donkey trembled and gave one huge

sigh. Then she lay quiet. But it wasn't quite over. There was something wrong. The foal wasn't breathing. The vet worked quickly. He rubbed the tiny body, massaging its chest and sides with a rough towel. Then he blew into the tiny nostrils.

'Breathe,' he murmured. 'Breathe.'

Suddenly the foal gasped and gave a shudder. Next minute it was struggling on to its side. Each breath was weak and shallow. But slowly the little donkey grew stronger.

The vet sank back onto his knees. 'It's a patchwork filly,' he grinned. 'A little girl.'

The next few moments were truly wonderful. Gingerly, the newborn foal struggled to get up. Her long, rubbery legs wobbled and collapsed as she tried again and again to stand.

Eventually she made it up on to all fours and rocked from side to side, blinking her huge eyes. Danni, Tim, and Kristie huddled together in admiration as the foal blew her first snort and nuzzled at her mother's flank looking for milk. But the mother lay very still. Sadly, the life she had given to her baby had tragically taken her own. The mother had died.

The isolation barn

The vet was in the barn with Danni, Peter, and Byron. That was the horse's name — Byron. Jenny had got that much information from Lance Parker when she drove him into Tarbrook. She'd also got him to sign a paper agreeing to sell Byron to The Sanctuary for £300 — the going rate for horse meat.

The vet had already bandaged the horse's leg and given him a painkilling injection, which seemed to be working nicely. Danni was feeding Byron slices of apple to take the horse's mind off his injuries. It was also giving Danni something constructive to do. Something to take her own mind off the donkey they had just lost. And the little orphaned foal.

'There, all done!' exclaimed the vet, trying to sound cheerful. The bandage looked enormous. 'I'm afraid he's going to have to stay immobile, here inside the stable, for at least a week. He needs a low protein diet and a course of antibiotic powders.'

'Staying here's no problem,' said Peter. 'But there might be a problem with keeping him inside. Apart from the injured leg, he's a fit, healthy horse. In a few days he'll be itching to get outside and stretch all four of them.'

Byron started nodding and rubbed his chin on the top of Danni's head. He was obviously a very nervy horse in need of some TLC. No way would the Lesters let him go to the knacker's yard. At that very moment, three donkeys poked their nosy heads over the half stable door. Houdini started lipping at the steel bolt, trying to slide it across the latch.

Dolly and Dolores, his two girlfriends, were stretching their necks, trying to lick Byron's handsome nose.

'Here comes the welcome committee,' grinned Peter, trying to lift the atmosphere.

Danni smiled, but she didn't really feel like smiling. She felt too sad for words. She spread her arms around the three donkeys and hugged their woolly necks. Danni felt like bursting into tears, but she didn't. She forced herself to be brave. When Danni grew up she wanted to be a vet. If she was going to help donkeys and spend happy days working at The Sanctuary, then she had to get used to sad days, too. But those days would never, ever be easy.

Early evening — The Sanctuary storerooms

Jenny and Kristie sat on bales of hay in an empty stall next to the tackroom. They'd scattered a thick bedding of sweet straw and made the little foal as comfortable as they could.

Jenny had her arms around the newborn, giving it affection and warmth. Overhead, a heatlamp glowed. At her feet lay a baby's bottle filled with a special milk mixture from the vet.

The gate-like door of the stall opened quietly as Danni slipped the latch. She stood there looking very concerned.

'How's Patches?' she asked softly. Danni had already named the baby foal.

Jenny shook her head. 'Not too good, I'm afraid. We've been trying to get her to take a bottle with milk and glucose. But the poor thing doesn't want to know.'

'We've managed to get a little down her,' added Kristie. 'Just enough to keep her alive. But what she really needs is her mother.'

The little foal looked as if she was sleeping peacefully in Jenny's arms. But as soon as she noticed Danni, Patches became instantly alert.

The little foal staggered away on unsteady legs and tried to hide behind a bale of hay.

'It's all right, baby,' soothed Danni. 'Come on, no one's going to harm you.' She held out her hand and coaxed the foal towards her. Danni couldn't take her eyes off little Patches. She was so beautiful. Almost silver-white in colour with black patches and one black-tipped ear. Her coat was soft and woolly. And her eyes were huge with curious wonder as she gazed at her loving admirers.

'Just look at her funny little mane,' whispered Danni. 'It's all bristly like a toothbrush.' The baby donkey was so sweet. Danni had never seen anything quite so beautiful.

But Patches was trembling from head to foot. Her long, thin legs were shaking so much that she could hardly stand.

Danni edged forward as slowly as she dared. She held out her hand for the foal to sniff. But the little donkey was nervous and timid, and shied away.

'Don't be scared, little one,' whispered Danni. She moved even closer and continued speaking in a soft, soothing voice.

The foal's nostrils twitched.

'She can smell the other donkeys on you,' smiled Jenny.

Patches relaxed, and finally Danni was able to touch her soft woolly coat. She stroked her neck and face while the foal sniffed at her clothes.

'Shall I try her with the bottle?' suggested Danni. 'Maybe I could get her to drink something.'

'She *must* start feeding properly, soon,' said Jenny. 'Or she'll be too weak to survive.'

Danni took the bottle and held it towards the

33

foal's mouth. At first Patches suckled. But then the little donkey lost interest and with a big sigh she pulled away and let go of the teat.

The following morning at The Sanctuary

Danni was running through the standard health checks which The Sanctuary performed daily on every single donkey in their care. Jenny and Kristie had stayed up all night, taking turns to sit with the newly born foal. Peter was with Patches now while Jenny and Kristie were resting. He was trying to coax the little donkey to feed. But like everyone else, he wasn't having much luck. Work at The Sanctuary had to carry on as normal, so Danni was going about all the regular chores as best as she could. She glanced at her watch. Tim would be there any minute to give her a hand.

Danni unclipped the lead rope from Jasper's head collar and let him loose in the exercise yard. Jasper was a bit of a hoover, and straight away started snuffling around looking for things to snack on. Anything would do . . . leaves, scraps of paper, the sleeve of Danni's sweatshirt as it hung over the fence rail.

Most of the other residents were grazing peacefully in the home field. All except Shadow, who was racing around the pasture at top speed, playing football with his best friend, Houdini.

Danni's little black racing donkey was brilliant at playing footy. He chased after Houdini like a dynamo, kicking and dribbling the ball away across the grassy paddock. Then suddenly he stopped midfield. He threw up his black, woolly head and hollered with his unique, ear-splitting bray. 'Hee hawwwww!!' Shadow's call was deafening. And just as well. For not only was Shadow the family pet, he was also The Sanctuary guard donkey. And he was telling Danni that someone was coming up the drive.

The other donkeys stopped munching grass

and looked up with their ears tick-tocking from side to side. They lined themselves up along the paddock fencing and set up a donkey chorus. Houdini picked up his feed bucket in his teeth and joined them.

Danni looked, too, with equal interest, as Jasper started eating the pocket of her jeans. The figure drew nearer. Then Danni's stomach did a somersault as she recognized the visitor. It was Lance Parker.

The main yard of The Sanctuary

Peter came out of the storeroom to see what all the commotion was about. It didn't take long to see that trouble was on its way.

'Where's my horse?' yelled Lance Parker even before he'd reached the main gate. 'I've changed my mind about selling him. I've come to take him away.'

Peter stood at the gate and refused Lance Parker entry.

'The Sanctuary's closed,' he informed him, firmly. 'And the cheque for Byron is in the post, recorded delivery. So you can just go away.'

'But I've changed my mind,' said Lance Parker again. 'I want my horse back.'

'Well, you know you can't have him,' responded Peter, calmly. 'The horse is injured and can't be moved. Besides, you agreed to sell him to us. We've paid your best price and you agreed to the sale. Byron belongs to us now. And he's staying here, in safety, at The Sanctuary. There's no more to be said.'

'I'll get my lawyers on to this!' threatened Lance Parker.

'And they'll tell you that when you signed this paper, you signed a legal document.' Jenny's voice rang loud and clear as she strode out of the farmhouse waving the contract of Byron's sale. 'Now, if you'll excuse us,' she added curtly, 'we have a very busy day ahead.'

Lance Parker grunted something under his breath and stormed off without looking back — which was just as well. Because, if he had

looked back, he would have seen Jasper snatch the contract from Jenny's hand and promptly swallow it whole.

The home paddock

Jenny decided to introduce Patches to a few of the residents. The little foal was already very curious about all the braying and other donkey noises she could hear outside. Danni agreed. She thought it was a great idea and hoped it would give Patches a bit more confidence if she met some grown-ups of her own kind.

With one hand resting gently on Patches' rump, Danni used a soft tea-towel wrapped loosely around the little foal's neck to lead Patches outside.

Queenie and Dixie were two of the oldest female residents at The Sanctuary. They were also two of the most gentle. Each had given birth to several foals in their lives before coming to live at Whistlewind Farm. Jenny hoped they might offer friendship and some comfort to the little orphaned Patches.

As soon as she set eyes on the two older donkeys, Patches's fluffy ears started waggling, like a rabbit's. And her long, stilt-like legs wobbled with excitement.

Queenie and Dixie crossed the paddock immediately to rub noses and nuzzle the little foal. Danni had made sure that they were the only two donkeys in the paddock. She released Patches to gambol freely, and laughed with Jenny as they watched the tiny donkey spring and dance in circles around the two adult mares.

Queenie and Dixie swung their heads, following the cheeky foal's antics. They made gentle, motherly braying sounds and licked the top of Patches's head as she nuzzled their flanks looking for milk.

But both Queenie and Dixie were dry. They had no milk for the little foal. It almost made things seem worse. Sadly, Danni realized that a foster mother with milk was the only way that Patches was going to feed properly. She decided that she had to do something. She had to help as much as she could. She was determined that,

somehow, she would find a foster mother for the little orphan. If she didn't, then Patches's chances of survival were very slim!

Whistlewind Farm — 5.30p.m. around the kitchen table

It had been a very long day. Danni had shared Patches's feeding rota with Jenny and Kristie. They each tried, for ten minutes every hour, to get the orphan to drink from the bottle. Each time, Patches fed a little. But each time she took barely enough to keep herself alive. Everyone was exhausted.

Now, Danni sat at the scrubbed pine table with an assortment of felt tipped pens and paper.

'There!' she exclaimed triumphantly. 'I've finished.' She sat back to admire her handiwork. Jenny and Peter looked over her shoulder to see what had been occupying Danni for the last hour.

Danni had made six posters. Each one read:

Danni had drawn a lovely picture of Patches next to The Sanctuary's telephone number.

'It's a great idea,' agreed Jenny.

'Worth a try,' added Peter. 'They're brilliant posters.'

'I thought I'd take Shadow out for a run after tea,' explained Danni. 'I'll do a circuit and stick up a few posters on the way. And I'll rope Tim in,' she added. 'He can stick up a few in Tarbrooke when he does his morning paper round.'

'Excellent,' said Peter. 'But don't stay out too long or go too far,' he told her. 'We don't need anything else to worry about at the moment.' Peter knew just how enthusiastic and headstrong his daughter could be. Especially when she was on a mission.

He also knew how fast Shadow could move when he was given his head. Shadow was a woolly dynamo, a super speed rocket who never seemed to get tired. Even when he was pulling his little fish cart, Shadow's ears pointed forward like lances, and his legs became no more than a blur as he galloped along.

But Danni wasn't planning on taking the cart. Shadow had his own saddle and full set of tack. She smiled to herself as she thought about it. Shadow could fly much faster without the buggy.

The isolation barn — the following morning

The vet was in the barn checking on Byron. The injured horse was on the mend and feeling restless. He didn't like being cooped up in the barn all day. But under the vet's orders he had to stay confined until the end of the week. Seven days full rest, until his leg had completely healed.

Byron was bobbing his head over the half stable door, waiting for his new friend, Houdini. Every day, the mischievous donkey came trotting across the exercise yard to pay a visit. Houdini rubbed noses with the horse, then began lipping at the door bolt — again.

'Stop that immediately!' warned Danni. She

was quite convinced that Houdini was really more interested in the door bolt than the horse inside the stable.

'If Houdini can't escape himself,' laughed Danni, 'then he seems determined to "spring" Byron.' She was still chuckling at her own joke when she suddenly heard a strange noise and noticed something going on in the wood just beyond the back field. The noise sounded a bit like a tractor. And . . . wait a minute. It wasn't the woods at all. Something was happening at the fence line to the field.

The back field

'Quick!' shouted Danni. 'The donkeys.' She dived over the rails into the back field. The donkeys there were going wild, trying to get away from the awful noise of the JCB.

It was soon clear what was happening. A mechanical digger was ripping up the post and rail fencing which bordered the back field,

45

separating The Sanctuary from the wood. Half
of it was already demolished.

'You catch the donkeys,' yelled Jenny,
bounding across the field. 'I'll stop the driver.'

Most of the donkeys had fled back and run
away from the noisy machine. But Captain,
Blue, and Rambo were braver than the rest.
They had already gone through the huge gap
and were deciding whether or not they could
jump the stream and reach the water marigolds
on the far bank. If the other donkeys saw them
and followed, they could all end up running

loose. And there was a main road on the other side of the wood.

'Stop!' Jenny threw herself in front of the JCB, waving her arms. 'Stop that at once!'

She quickly coaxed Captain, Blue, and Rambo back to the safety of the field. Fence rails and broken posts were strewn everywhere. It looked as if a herd of elephants had just charged through.

'What's your problem, lady?' The driver of the JCB growled in a deep gravelly voice. He looked as though he could rip up the fencing with his bare hands.

'Just what on earth do you think you're doing?' yelled Jenny. She sounded furious.

'I'm just doing my job,' reported the driver. 'I'm doing exactly what my boss has instructed me to do.'

'Are you crazy? You're pulling down our fence,' screamed Jenny. 'I'm calling the police.'

'Call who you like,' replied the driver. 'This is Redbourne Paxton land. It might be your fence but it's their boundary. If Redbourne

Paxton Estates want your fence taken off their land then down it comes.'

'But you can't just leave us with no fence,' said Jenny.

'That's your problem, I'm afraid,' answered the driver. 'I'm only obeying orders. Now if you don't mind, I'd like to get back to work and finish the job.'

Jenny couldn't believe what was happening. And there was nothing that she could do about it. Jenny rang the police *and* Redbourne Paxton Estates. But they only confirmed what the driver had told her. The boundary line did belong to RP Estates. And they were perfectly within their rights to pull down the fence. The new manager had issued the order. But why would he do such a thing? Jenny was determined to find out.

The exercise yard

Danni had opened the gate and driven the donkeys through from the back field into the exercise yard. Surprisingly, Houdini made no attempt to slip through and escape. Instead, the mischievous donkey was preoccupying himself with all the locks and bolts on the stable doors. One door in particular held Houdini's interest more than the others. The last stable in the block. In fact, it wasn't used as a real stable any more. It was used as a store and tackroom. The bolt on this door was nice and loose. Houdini had no trouble at all in lipping the latch and sliding the bolt across. The door was easy to nose open. Houdini wandered inside.

Inside the stable was a stall with another door to open. This door was no more than a gate. Today was Houdini's lucky day. No one seemed to notice little Patches as she slipped out into the exercise yard. There were so many fully grown donkeys, pushing and milling around. So many strange smells and noises. Patches wasn't quite sure where she was. She nuzzled as many flanks as she could, going from one donkey to another, hoping to find her mother's milk. But all the donkeys were dry and moved away briskly.

49

Then Patches found Tina. Tina was a younger, more boisterous donkey. In fact she was also a bit of a hooligan. Tina didn't like this strange little foal pushing and butting at her soft, round belly. She didn't like it one bit. So she nipped the little foal's legs.

Patches was both shocked and surprised. It made her jump. It frightened her. She had never been nipped before. It didn't feel friendly. Patches ran. She ran and ran on her long rubbery legs. And no one noticed her disappear. She was so tiny. And everyone was busy with all the fussing and confusion over the fence.

It was some time before Patches was found to be missing.

Midday — the store-room

Peter was outside, frantically hammering and

re-siting the fence posts on Sanctuary land while Jenny checked on all the residents.

Danni had just given Byron a special powder from the vet concealed in a hollowed out apple. It was the only way that the horse would take his medicine without making a terrible fuss. He was crunching his apple greedily when Jenny was suddenly calling.

'Where is she? What's happened to Patches?' Jenny's voice rang, worried and concerned, across the exercise yard. 'Patches has gone. She's not in her stable. Where is she?'

Danni closed the stable door and hurried outside to see what was going on. Jenny was standing there holding Patches's feed bottle, running an anxious hand through her short hair. Danni had never seen her mother look so worried.

'The stable door was wide open,' said Jenny. 'Patches couldn't have opened it herself!'

'It wasn't me,' said Danni, defensively.

Jenny managed a smile. 'Oh, I'm not blaming you, darling. It's just that someone *must* have opened the door and let her out. I can't imagine any other way.'

Danni thought carefully for a moment.

'I bet it was while we were all busy out in the back field,' she said. 'While we were all occupied and looking out for the donkeys. Someone must have crept in and opened the stable door. I bet it was that nasty Lance Parker!'

Jenny was mulling over the possibility when Houdini edged close and nudged at the feed bottle in her hand. Peter came in from the field just as Danni and Jenny exchanged quick glances.

'You don't think . . .' began Danni. She watched Houdini trying to suck the teat.

'It's more than possible,' said Jenny, picking up Danni's thoughts. 'It wouldn't surprise me one bit if Houdini here was the culprit.'

'Was it you, boy?' asked Danni. She lowered her face and looked Houdini right in the eye. 'Did you let Patches out of her stable?'

Somehow, the donkey seemed to understand. Houdini looked so guilty. He lowered his head

in shame and delivered a series of huffy little blows. Then he tried to hide behind Peter.

'He obviously did,' said Danni. 'Just look at him!'

'And now we've got to find her,' exclaimed Jenny. 'Patches won't survive for long out there on her own.'

Peter quickly realized what had happened.

'Maybe she's still here, hiding somewhere in The Sanctuary,' he suggested. 'Let's check all the barns and stables.'

After a long search they found nothing.

'I'll saddle up Shadow,' said Danni. 'We'll scout the woods and marshlands.'

'I'll take the Range Rover,' said Jenny. Her voice sounded urgent. 'I can cover most of Tarr Downs while Dad looks after things here. Patches may come back and there's the other residents to think of.'

Within minutes they were all going about their individual missions. But hours later, they were all back sitting at the kitchen table with long faces and heavy hearts.

'There was no sign of Patches anywhere,' said Jenny.

'I checked all the outbuildings twice. The fields and the lanes,' said Peter.

'We combed the woods three times,' said Danni. 'Wherever Patches is, she isn't there.'

Suddenly the kitchen door flew open and Tim burst in, all red faced and out of breath. He had been pedalling like mad all the way from Tarbrooke.

'Look at these!' complained Tim. He spread

a pile of crumpled papers across the table. 'Look what's happened to our posters! Someone's ripped them all down.' He went on to explain. 'I was just on my way over, when I noticed one of the posters I'd pinned up was torn and hanging from the fence. I decided to check on the others and found them all torn and ripped, just like the first one.'

Danni was shocked. Then Jenny told Tim about the business with The Sanctuary fence and how Patches had vanished. Tim's chin almost hit the table.

'I'll go back home the long way,' he offered, 'and keep my eyes peeled for any sign of her.'

'Thanks,' said Danni. 'I'm going out with Dad in the truck for another look. Maybe we might be lucky this time!'

The next morning

Everyone at The Sanctuary was up extra early. Danni knew that if Patches wasn't found today, then the chances of her surviving any longer were very slim. Without milk, the little foal would be too weak to last more than another day.

Danni wanted to get all the feeds out of the way nice and early and go looking for Patches again.

Jenny had hoped that maybe the baby donkey would have found her way back home. But it was wishful thinking. Patches hadn't turned up.

All the other donkeys at The Sanctuary seemed to sense that something was wrong. Some were still distressed by the events of the day before, with the noisy JCB ripping out their fence. And being unable to use the big back field had upset their routine and made conditions a bit cramped. A big heavy cloud hung over The Sanctuary like a dark cloak.

As much as Jenny wanted to join the search party, she still had a sanctuary to run. Each resident needed a daily health check. And this morning, most needed an extra serving of TLC.

Jenny would go looking for Patches again once Kristie had turned up and all The Sanctuary duties were completed. Peter wanted to finish the fencing by lunchtime and get things running back to normal as quickly as possible. So that left Danni and Tim, heading the final search party.

The Sanctuary gates

Danni saddled up Houdini for Tim to ride. She had this crazy notion that maybe Houdini could lead them to Patches. After all, he *had* been very curious about the little foal. And he *did* seem to be feeling guilty about letting her out. Danni thought it was worth a try.

'Where shall we look first?' asked Tim. He opened the big gate for Danni and Shadow to pass through.

'I know it sounds daft,' began Danni, 'but why don't we just let Houdini lead the way. He's always trying to get out and escape, isn't he! So let's just give him his head and see where he goes. He might just lead us to Patches.'

Tim raised his eyebrows questioningly. But Houdini was very happy to oblige. As usual, Shadow wanted to dash ahead. The black racing donkey pumped his little legs up and down on the spot with excitement. But Danni held him back and let Tim and Houdini walk ahead.

Houdini sniffed the fresh morning air. Then he blew a delighted, rumbling snort as he sensed the slack reins. His long ears tick-tocked from

side to side. Houdini was off, trotting away on a determined course towards Sunset Cliffs.

'I didn't check the clifftops before,' said Danni. 'I didn't think there would be anything there to attract a baby donkey. It's all barren rock . . .'

'. . . and steep drops into the ocean,' concluded Tim, morbidly, as he finished her sentence.

Danni fell silent. Suddenly she felt too sick with worry to speak.

Houdini charged on ahead. He seemed to be heading directly for the clifftop path. But then, at the last possible moment, he changed direction and headed off down a small cart-path that ran parallel to the River Tarr and the road to Redlands.

Danni and Shadow followed behind. Danni thought that she knew all the local paths and bridleways. But this cart-path was new to both Tim *and* Danni.

Minutes later it wasn't even a path any more. A muddy track would have described it better. A muddy track which suddenly came to an abrupt end at a line of tall, silver trees.

'This track doesn't lead anywhere!' protested Tim. 'At first, I thought it was a shortcut into Redlands. But Houdini has led us on a wild-goose chase.'

They were about to turn back when Houdini dug in his heels. And when a donkey does that, neither heaven nor earth will make it move. Houdini looked towards his friend Shadow for support. He blew a wheezing bray. The two donkeys suddenly became very excited about something. They were both sniffing at the air and snorting to each other, donkey fashion.

Danni slipped from the saddle and walked Shadow up to the line of trees. Their silver leaves glimmered in the sunshine. And to her surprise, the track didn't end there at all.

A slight rise in the earth approaching the trees was hiding what lay beyond. Danni stood in the leafy shadows and gazed down across a green, shallow basin. She was looking at the red-tiled roof of a small, stone cottage. There was also a large barn, some outbuildings, a large vegetable plot with a shed. And a small paddock behind the cottage itself. Everything looked so neat and tidy, just like a perfect photograph in one of Jenny's country magazines.

'What is it?' called Tim.

'Come and take a look at this,' enthused Danni. 'I don't know exactly *why* Houdini has led us here. But it looks like a very secret and special place.'

Tim looked down at the picturesque homestead below.

'Wow! I wonder who lives there.'

'Let's find out,' said Danni.

They led their donkeys down the narrow, winding path. The tiny hairs on the back of Danni's neck stood on end. There was an unexpected excitement in the air. It felt electric.

Both Shadow and Houdini could feel it too. Houdini was 'hawing' softly and nodding his woolly head up and down. Then Shadow started braying quite loudly. He was also desperately trying to push his way in front and race ahead down the slope.

As they drew nearer, Danni and Tim could see chickens roosting in the lower branches of an old apple tree. There were two goats dozing in the sun-dappled shadows. A big ginger cat lay curled on the cottage doorstep. And in the paddock, Danni saw . . . two donkeys. And a foal.

The Sanctuary

Jenny rolled Captain's top lip back and checked the donkey's teeth. She turned to Kristie.

'Make an entry against Captain's health notes,' she said. 'His teeth need rasping on the vet's next visit.' Donkeys sometimes develop sharp points on their teeth which can cause them pain and problems if they're not treated early enough. Most donkeys enjoy the filing sensation of 'rasping'. They seem to understand that it's for their own good. Captain was no exception.

Kristie made a note on the donkey's sheet.

'Right then. That's all the health checks finished,' she announced.

Jenny checked her watch. It was ten thirty.

'Well, seeing that Danni finished all the feeds nice and early,' said Jenny. 'We can now go and join the search for little Patches.' Jenny knew it might be their last chance.

'I'll just grab my jacket,' said Kristie. But Jenny and Kristie weren't going anywhere just yet. Suddenly a familiar yet unwelcome voice rang in their ears.

'I want a copy of that so-called "contract of sale",' bellowed Lance Parker. He was making

63

himself heard again, loud and clear. 'I've spoken to my solicitor this morning, and he wants to see a copy of that so-called document, which you're using to swindle me out of my horse.'

Jenny felt her blood boil. There was something about Lance Parker which made her skin prickle.

'I haven't got time for this!' snapped Jenny. 'I'm just on my way out.'

'Well, I demand a copy of that contract,' roared Lance Parker. 'And I'm not leaving until I get it.'

Jenny suddenly remembered that Jasper had eaten it. There was no contract. Only an exchange of money.

'I sent you a cheque for three hundred pounds,' said Jenny, as she made her way to the Range Rover. 'It's what we agreed. That cheque is proof enough,' she bluffed. 'Proof enough to anyone that you have sold Byron to The Sanctuary.'

'I haven't cashed that cheque,' sneered Lance Parker. 'My solicitor says that cheque doesn't prove a thing without a contract. And as far as I'm concerned, I want my horse returned.'

'Well you can't have him,' concluded Jenny. She slammed the car door and started the engine.

'He looks like he's going to explode,' whispered Kristie.

'Good,' Jenny retorted. 'Then he looks exactly like how I feel. The cheek of the man.'

The Range Rover screeched noisily down the drive, spitting gravel from the tyres.

'He's right about the cheque though, isn't he?' asked Kristie. 'If he hasn't cashed it then there's been no sale. And as we haven't got the contract any more, we can't prove anything, can we!'

'I know,' said Jenny worriedly. 'I'll have to think of something.'

Kristie checked the rear-view mirror. Lance Parker was staring after them and waving his arms in the air like a lunatic.

'Better think of something good,' said Kristie. 'For Byron's sake!'

Redburn Hollow

The little stone cottage was as pretty as a picture. Thick ivy clung to the white-washed walls and wound its way up and over the red-tiled roof. The door to the cottage was ajar. The fat ginger cat on the doorstep watched them with great interest. The goats stirred. And the hens in the apple tree ruffled their feathers. Danni's eyes sparkled at the thrill of being there. It was as though they had stumbled across some secret, magical place which had been forgotten and buried away in the countryside for centuries.

As the pathway levelled out, Shadow and Houdini put on a spurt. Each seemed to be trying to get there before the other. They were just as keen as Danni and Tim to get to the cottage and the paddock behind it.

The air was still and quiet. Then the braying began. The two donkeys in the paddock caught Shadow's and Houdini's scent. They poked their shaggy heads over the top rail of the paddock fence and began braying a loud welcome.

Shadow was the first to answer. The little black donkey threw back his head and opened his lungs. The noise which came out was truly deafening. They could probably have heard it all the way back at The Sanctuary.

Houdini immediately joined in the chorus. And before Danni knew what was happening, the cottage door flew open and an old man rushed out into the garden.

Tarr Downs

Jenny and Kristie had been driving around for hours, combing the countryside. They tried to think of all the unlikely places where Patches could be trapped or hiding. They had already checked out the most *likely* places, and found nothing. Patches seemed to have disappeared off the face of the earth.

They were just about ready to return to The Sanctuary, when Jenny drove past the Redbourne Paxton Offices. The RP Estate

Management Offices were no more than a small lodge, set back on the Tarr Road to Dunnisford.

Without really thinking, Jenny pulled up and parked outside the building.

'I'll only be a tick,' she said. 'There's something I want to clear up.'

Minutes later Jenny came out of the lodge with a face like thunder.

'You'll never guess who's the new Estate Manager,' she exclaimed.

'You mean the person responsible for pulling down our fence?' replied Kristie.

'Exactly. That very same person.'

Kristie didn't have a clue.

Jenny's brows knitted themselves together into a very deep frown as she supplied the answer.

'Lance Parker!'

Redburn Hollow

At first, Danni and Tim felt awkward. The old

man looked quite cross as he stood in his garden. After all, Danni and Tim *were* trespassing. They didn't mean any harm, but they *had* walked, with two donkeys, down to the man's cottage, uninvited.

There was no need to worry, though. As soon as the old man saw Shadow and Houdini, his face softened. Like Danni and Tim, he clearly had a great love of donkeys.

Danni took a deep breath and tried to explain everything very quickly without gulping too much air or burping. It turned out that the old man knew all about The Sanctuary.

He listened. And smiled.

'So you thought that maybe your little orphan foal might be hiding here?' he said. 'I don't get many visitors, so a little foal would be very welcome.'

But the old man added that he hadn't seen Patches. Or the posters that Danni and Tim had put up. Then he looked really sad and explained how his own two donkeys, Bonnie and Clyde, had recently lost their own new-born foal.

'I could have phoned you at The Sanctuary,' he said, 'had I known about Patches.'

Danni glanced at Tim. She didn't like to say anything, but she was almost certain that she had seen a baby donkey in the paddock behind the cottage.

Shadow reached forward and butted the old man playfully on the arm. Then he nosed at his pockets looking for a treat.

'He's a cheeky one, isn't he,' laughed the old man as he stroked Shadow's black, woolly neck.

Danni couldn't have chosen a better moment.

'Can we say hello to Bonnie and Clyde?' she asked, hoping for a closer look at the paddock. If Patches was hiding back there, then Danni wasn't leaving until she had taken a good look.

Houdini didn't wait for an answer. He suddenly lurched forward and pulled Tim around the side of the cottage.

Clyde was happy to meet Shadow and Houdini. The donkeys rubbed noses over the fence and exchanged donkey greetings. Bonnie, on the other hand, seemed shy. She turned on her heels and hurried into her stable.

Danni had a good look around the paddock while Tim fussed over Clyde. But there was no sign of Patches, or any other baby donkey.

Eventually, Danni just came right out with it and said to the old man, 'I thought I saw a foal, earlier. It was in the paddock with the two donkeys.'

The old man seemed genuinely surprised.

'I think you must have been mistaken,' he

remarked, sadly. 'There's no foal here. Bonnie's little baby died last week. She's only just starting to get over it.'

But he told Danni that she was welcome to have a good look around if she wanted. There was a barn. Several outbuildings. And a block of stables.

'I suppose it is possible that your little donkey could have found her way here,' he admitted. 'But I would have thought that I would have seen something of her, if she had!'

Then he offered to help Danni and Tim search the entire homestead while Shadow and Houdini played football with Clyde.

The isolation barn — The Sanctuary

Jenny petted Byron's arched neck. 'So how did you get caught up with that nasty Lance Parker?' she whispered.

The gentle horse lipped at Jenny's collar and blew hot air down her neck. He whickered

softly and listened calmly to her soothing tones.
'I don't know if we are going to be able to keep
you, after all,' said Jenny. 'But we won't give
you up without a fight. And I promise you that
you won't ever go to any knackers yard.'

When Jenny returned to The Sanctuary with
Kristie, Peter had told her about Lance Parker's
visit. Lance Parker had stayed behind when
Jenny had driven off earlier. He had threatened
to sue The Sanctuary. He also said that he
would do everything in his power to destroy
Whistlewind Farm, if he didn't have his horse
returned. He was calling back at five o'clock to
sort it all out once and for all.

Now that Jenny and Peter knew Lance
Parker was the new RP Estates Manager, and
responsible for most of the surrounding land
and properties, they had to take his threat
seriously. Lance Parker could close bridlepaths
and access to The Sanctuary where private
roads crossed RP fields. And the stream which
supplied spring water to Whistlewind Farm and
The Sanctuary paddocks also bubbled beyond

their boundary on RP land. Yes! Lance Parker could cause lots of problems.

If only Jasper hadn't eaten that contract. Lance Parker wouldn't have had a leg to stand on in any court of law. Peter didn't think they had much of a choice but to hand Byron over, once his injuries were completely healed.

And for once in her life, Jenny didn't know what to do about it!

Redburn Hollow — The donkey stables

'Well I never,' exclaimed the old man. They had checked all the barns and all the outbuildings. Now they stood in the doorway of Bonnie and Clyde's stable.

Danni grinned at Tim. Then she smiled at Bonnie — and the little patchwork foal, nuzzling and suckling at the donkey's tummy.

'I don't believe it!' The old man's eyes brimmed with tears. It was such a wonderful sight. Bonnie was braying a soft lullaby and

licking the tips of little Patches's ears. The two lost souls had both found each other. And it was truly beautiful.

'The foal looks healthy,' smiled the old man. 'Bonnie must have been feeding her ever since she ran away from The Sanctuary. I wondered why she kept rushing off and disappearing into her stable every five minutes. I thought she was just missing her baby, so I left her alone for some peace and grieving time.'

Patches suckled her fill of milk, then came

trotting across the straw to greet Danni and Tim. Danni gave the little foal a big hug and kissed her tufty forelock. The baby donkey blinked her long dark lashes and brayed a shrill snort of excitement. Then she bounced back to Bonnie.

'They look made for each other,' beamed Danni. 'I think they've bonded.'

'That's exactly what I was thinking,' said the old man. 'Mother and daughter.'

The Sanctuary — 4.45p.m.

Danni and Tim came trotting up The Sanctuary drive on Shadow and Houdini. Riding between them was the old man from Redburn Hollow on his donkey, Clyde.

The old man had told them to call him Bill — short for William.

Bill had come along to The Sanctuary to talk with Jenny and Peter about Patches. As his own donkey Bonnie had just lost her own foal, and as Patches was in desperate need of a foster mother, it seemed like the ideal solution if

Patches could stay at Redburn Hollow. The little foal could be adopted and grow up as part of a real donkey family.

Jenny and Peter were just coming out of Byron's stable as the three donkeys and their riders opened the big gate and entered the exercise yard.

Jenny could tell by Danni's face that there was good news coming.

Bill introduced himself. Then Danni blurted everything out as quickly as one breath would allow.

Jenny and Peter were thrilled to hear that Patches was safe and sound. They were also pleased to learn that she had found a foster mother. And was at last suckling milk, naturally, from Bill's mare.

'If only you'd seen Danni's posters,' said Jenny, 'Patches and Bonnie could have been introduced days ago.'

Danni reminded everyone that someone had ripped all the posters down.

'That's why no one called The Sanctuary,'

she said. 'That rotten Lance Parker made sure of that!'

Bill cocked his head to one side at the mention of Lance Parker's name.

Jenny raised a disapproving eyebrow.

'Now, Danni . . .' she said. 'As much as I don't like the man, we don't really know for certain that it was him.'

'I bet it was,' grumbled Danni. 'And I'll tell him just what I think, next time I see him!'

'You'll do no such thing,' warned Jenny. 'We don't want any more unpleasantness. Especially now, when it looks as though we've got to let him take Byron back.'

Jenny explained everything to their visitor. And Bill seemed absolutely astonished at the tale. He listened very carefully indeed.

'Can I see the injured horse?' he asked.

Jenny nodded her approval and Peter led him to Byron's stable.

Seconds later, Lance Parker slammed the door of his flashy car and marched up the drive into The Sanctuary. It was exactly 5 o'clock.

Jenny, who never missed a trick, saw him coming. She asked Tim to take care of the donkeys and lead Shadow, Houdini, and Clyde, away from the exercise yard.

'I've got a letter here of my own,' bellowed Lance Parker. 'It's from my solicitor.' He waved a white envelope as he approached. 'If this nonsense isn't settled today, I'll be suing you in court, for every penny you've got!'

'There'll be no need for that,' said Jenny, calmly. It was the first time she had ever felt totally defeated. 'You can have Byron,' she said. 'But there are three conditions,' she added. 'One — Byron stays here until he is one hundred per cent fit and his leg is completely healed. Two — you forget any ideas of selling him for horse-meat. And three — you leave The Sanctuary alone!'

Lance Parker just stood there and laughed. 'You're in no position to make demands,' he sneered. 'That horse is mine. And I'll do whatever I like with it. And as for this pathetic sanctuary . . .' Lance Parker's voice suddenly trailed off. He never got to finish his sentence.

Bill came out of Byron's stable with Peter and met Lance Parker eye to eye.

'Hello, Lance,' Bill said coolly.

Lance Parker's mouth dropped open as he gulped air. Danni thought that he looked like a bloated goldfish.

'Mr Redddddbourne,' was all he managed to stammer.

'Do you two know each other?' asked Jenny, rather puzzled by Lance Parker's reaction.

Bill smiled. 'This is the young man who is hoping to marry my granddaughter and come into the family business,' he said, rather frostily. Lance Parker suddenly looked very anxious.

'Mr Parker here,' began Bill, 'has been appointed acting manager of Redbourne Paxton Estates. He's got three months to prove himself to me and the family board of directors.'

Jenny looked even more puzzled.

Bill smiled kindly and explained. 'I live in a small cottage in the middle of nowhere because I now choose to live that way. Since my wife died, five years ago, I've never wanted to live anywhere else. It was our special place. Our secret retreat.' Bill was happy living on his own with his memories and his animals.

Jenny suddenly realized exactly who Bill was. Of course . . . he was Mr Redbourne — head of the family who owned RP Estates.

Lance Parker was virtually quaking in his boots. Big bully-boy was suddenly put in his place by the presence of this little, friendly, old man called Bill.

Mr Redbourne — or Bill — took the letter that Lance Parker had been brandishing and tore it up into tiny pieces. Jasper was there in seconds, trying to hoover up the tasty scraps.

'Don't let him eat paper,' called Jenny. Danni got most of it away from him. But not before the scavenging donkey had chewed a few pieces.

Bill sent Lance Parker on his way with his tail between his legs.

'You'll have no more trouble from him, I promise you,' said Bill. 'We'll be keeping a very close eye on that young man from now on. He's got a lot to learn. And a lot to prove.'

Everyone breathed a big sigh of relief.

'I'd also like to offer a permanent home to Byron, once he's recovered,' Bill continued. 'He'll be in good company at Redburn Hollow. And you can come and visit him whenever you like.'

It sounded like a great idea. There wasn't really room for a horse at The Sanctuary. Especially a lively one like Byron, who would need lots of exercise.

'There's a huge, quiet field next to the paddock,' said Bill. 'Perfect for a horse like Byron. And plenty of stabling.'

Jenny was nodding her head and smiling.

'And Patches,' chirped Danni. 'What about Patches? She's found Bonnie now. And at long last, she's feeding properly. Can she stay at Redburn Hollow, too?'

Jenny was tempted to say 'yes' straight

away. Naturally, she had Patches's best interests at heart. And she was thrilled about the offer to adopt Byron. She didn't want to appear ungrateful, but Jenny wanted to see Redburn Hollow for herself before she committed to anything.

Bill understood completely. He was such a nice man.

Redburn Hollow — the following day

The little patchwork foal gambolled around the paddock like a frisky lamb. Bonnie watched her every move. She lowered her head and brayed softly each time Patches bounced past.

'She's an excellent foster mother,' praised Bill.

'I can see that,' smiled Jenny. 'She's brilliant!'

Patches had filled out quite a bit since Jenny had last seen her. She looked fit and healthy. 'There's nothing like a mother's milk,' she added.

Danni laughed as the little foal found a
dusty patch in the green pasture to roll in.
Patches lay on her back and kicked her long,
skinny legs in the air while Bonnie bellowed
her donkey approval. 'Heeehaawwwww!
Heeehaawwwww!' Clyde looked on proudly at
his new family. It was such a lovely moment.

'She looks very settled,' observed Jenny. 'In
fact, she looks perfectly at home, here at
Redburn Hollow.'

'I was hoping you'd say that,' smiled Bill.
'We'd love to have Patches here.'

Danni looked up at Jenny. But she could
already see by her mother's huge grin that the
answer was going to be 'yes'.

Patches came bounding over and slipped right through the paddock fencing. She stepped easily between the wooden rails and stood on the grass in front of them.

Danni bent down and gave the little foal a big hug and a kiss.

'You can come and see her whenever you like,' offered Bill.

Everything had turned out fine.

As Jenny and Danni left for home, they both had eyes brimming with tears. They looked at each other in the car, and laughed. It was a happy time.

Other books in the series

Donkey Danger
ISBN 0 19 275122 0

Danni's parents run a donkey sanctuary at their home on Whistlewind Farm and there's nothing Danni and her friend, Tim, enjoy more than helping to look after all the donkeys. But the sanctuary is short of funds so Danni decides to do a sponsored point-to-point with Shadow, her racing donkey.

As they journey around the local countryside Danni meets several people who tell her about a new donkey retirement home. But there's something about their stories that worries Danni. Who is the strange man who is buying up all the local donkeys? And where exactly is this mystery retirement home?

Donkey Disaster

ISBN 0 19 275123 9

The donkey sanctuary at Whistlewind Farm has started a bed and breakfast service to raise some funds. The first guests at the Farm are Robyn Springer and her mother. Robyn loves the farm and spends all her time helping out with the donkeys, but unfortunately her mother is not so keen on getting herself mucky!

But when Mrs Springer learns about a plan to build a factory in the field next to the sanctuary, she is determined to do all she can to keep the donkeys safe and the field free from development.

Donkey Drama
ISBN 0 19 275124 7

Danni and her friend Tim are horrified to learn that a blind donkey is being kept in terrible conditions, so, together with Danni's mother, they decide to rescue the donkey and give him a new home at Whistlewind Farm.

The donkey soon becomes friends with Tina, the sanctuary's most fiery resident, and has an amazing, calming effect on her. So much so that when the local theatre company call at the sanctuary looking for a donkey to star in their latest production, it seems Tina could be the natural choice.